Green Light Readers
For the new reader who's ready to GO!

Amazing adventures await every young child who is eager to read.
Green Light Readers encourage children to explore, to imagine, and to grow
through books. Created for beginning readers at two levels of skill, these lively illustrated
stories have been carefully developed to reinforce reading basics taught at school and
to make reading a fun and rewarding experience for children and grown-ups to share
outside the classroom.

The grades and ages within each skill level are general guidelines only, and books
included in both levels may feature any or all of the bulleted characteristics. When
choosing a book for a new reader, remember that every child progresses at his or her
own pace—be patient and supportive as the magic of reading takes hold.

❶ Buckle up!
Kindergarten–Grade 1: Developing reading skills, ages 5–7
- Short, simple stories • Fully illustrated • Familiar objects and situations
- Playful rhythms • Spoken language patterns of children
- Rhymes and repeated phrases • Strong link between text and art

2 Start the engine!
Grades 1–2: Reading with help, ages 6–8
- Longer stories, including nonfiction • Short chapters
- Generously illustrated • Less-familiar situations
- More fully developed characters • Creative language, including dialogue
- More subtle link between text and art

*Green Light Readers incorporate characteristics detailed in the Reading Recovery model
used by educators to assess the readability of texts through the end of first grade.
Guidelines for reading levels for these readers have been developed with assistance from
Mary Lou Meerson. An educational consultant, Ms. Meerson has been a classroom teacher,
a language arts coordinator, an elementary school principal, and a university professor.*

Published in collaboration with Harcourt Brace School Publishers

POPCORN

Alex Moran
Illustrated by Betsy Everitt

Green Light Readers
Harcourt Brace & Company
San Diego   New York   London

First Green Light Readers edition 1999
Green Light Readers is a trademark of Harcourt Brace & Company.

The Library of Congress has cataloged the original paperback edition as follows:
Moran, Alex.
Popcorn/Alex Moran; illustrated by Betsy Everitt.
p.   cm.
"Green Light Readers."
Summary: Illustrations and rhythmic, rhyming text show what happens
when popping popcorn gets out of hand.
[1. Popcorn—Fiction.   2. Stories in rhyme.]   I. Everitt, Betsy, ill.   II. Title.
PZ8.3.M795Po   1999
[E]—dc21   98-15566
ISBN 0-15-201998-7 (pb)

ISBN 0-15-202375-5

D F G E C (pb)

C E F D B

Printed in Hong Kong

Popcorn. Popcorn.

Put it in a pot.

Popcorn. Popcorn.

Get the pot hot.

Popcorn. Popcorn.
Put in lots more.

Popcorn. Popcorn.
One, two, three, four.

Popcorn. Popcorn.
Pop! Pop! Pop!

Popcorn. Popcorn.
Stop! Stop! Stop!

Popcorn. Popcorn.
What is the plan?

Popcorn. Popcorn.
Catch it if you can!

Popcorn. Popcorn.
It's going out the door.

Popcorn. Popcorn.
Stop! No more!

Popcorn. Popcorn.
Get it while it's hot.

**Look for these other Green Light Readers—
all affordably priced in paperback!**

Green Light Readers is a trademark of Harcourt Brace & Company.

Green Light Readers
For the new reader who's ready to GO!

We are happy.
We like it a lot!

Meet the Illustrator

Betsy Everitt likes to go to the movies and get a big bucket of popcorn. She and her family like to make popcorn at home, too.

Betsy Everitt chose animals with nice shapes and used lots of bright colors for this story. She put the colors and shapes together to create feelings. How do you feel when you look at her pictures?

Dale Higgins

BETSY EVERITT